With Love

and

Peace

Carolee O'Neill

Chocolate

Book has been handcrafted from cover to cover,
including the watercolor illustrations by Carolee.

From Silly to Sinister

Short Story Collection

Book One

original copyrights © from 1997 to 2011

Compiled in 2011

Copyrights © are owned by "The Carolee O'Neill Collection."

ISBN:978-1-947573-05-5

Library of Congress Catalog Card Number: 2017950116

The Carolee Collectables
Printed in the United States of America
www.crystalsforkids.org

Carolee O'Neill
http://books2c4kids.com

Carolee O'Neill

Acknowledgements

To all my friends and family who willingly gave of their time to edit the stories of my twelve books; patiently taught me computer jargon; shared their computer skills with Adobe InDesign and Photoshop; and guided me through the copyright, ISBN and barcode maze. I couldn't have done it without you.

Title

A Cane with a Name

The Long Journey Home

Lace Curtains

Knock on Heaven's Door

On the Road Again

Tall Tales

The Latest Guest

Sinister Secrets

Carolee O'Neill

From Silly to Sinister

Book One

Short Story Collection

To:

_____

_____

From:

_____

_____

Carolee O'Neill

Dedicated to David,

whose courage and laughter

will always be in my heart.

A Cane with a Name

It had been a long day for Mr. Phillips, the administrator of his hundred bed nursing home. His social worker had taken the week off so he would have to cover for her and do all the admissions. Although assuming necessary duties for vacationing department heads was not an uncommon practice in a small home, it became tedious for him on top of all of his other responsibilities. Luckily, he only had one more couple to place, and they were married.

This shouldn't be too tough. All I have to do is move a few residents to where there is an empty bed. That will free up some space so I can put this new couple together in the same room. I'm sure that after sixty years of marriage they are used to cuddling. Unfortunately, all we can do is push their beds together. At least they'll be able to hold hands, if nothing else.

"Come in," Mr. Phillips said when the nursing assistant knocked.

Molly, the elderly woman who Mary pushed into the room in a wheelchair, gripped a cane she called, Myrtle. Behind them hobbled a man supported by a walker.

Mr. Phillip jumped to his feet, "Good afternoon, folks! Here, sir, take my chair until Mary can bring another one."

Smiling sheepishly, Joe's legs trembled as he began to sit down.

"I have everything set for you," Mr. Phillips said as though he had just won the Nobel Prize. "Just give me a moment to finalize things in the computer,"

Being bored with the routine, Molly falls asleep.

Realizing this, Mr. Phillip went around to the front of his desk to be closer to the couple. Then he lowered his voice, so he wouldn't startle Molly.

"Here, I'll show you on this map of the home where your room is located."

Molly's eye's pop open, "Did I hear you say your room?"

"Yes Ma'am. We moved some people around so you and your husband could be together."

Molly poked Mr. Phillip in the chest with Myrtle, emphasizing each word with each jab. "Well, you just better get busy and move them back."

Then Molly swung Myrtle at Joe. He ducked and raised his arms in defense. In a flash, Molly found a opening for Myrtle to get in another jab when Joe left his guard down for a second.

Molly cackled her delight.

Mr. Phillips moved quickly behind his desk, trying to maintain his professionalism.

Finished with Joe, Molly turned her attention back toward Mr. Phillips."Let me tell you something, Mister. I'm not spending one more minute with this autocratic, superficial old goat. All day long, I'm either chopping food to put down his gullet or crushing pills so he can swallow them. And just like all fuddy-duddies, his list of medications are as long as my arm. For over fifty years, we've nurtured this war and now you're telling me it's going to continue?" she barked.

Mr. Phillips stuttered, "N-No Ma'am, I was. . ."

Molly brought Myrtle straight down, hitting the floor with a thud! "The war is over, Mister! And I've decided to become a civilian. It's time Myrtle and I had our own space. You'd better get busy, Mister, and play Chinese Checkers with those old people. 'Cuz this old lady wants a room of her own.

"Yes Ma'am. We'll surely do that, " Mr. Phillips said as he flopped into his chair with a sighed.

"Now that's a deal I can live with," Joe said. "A room of my own. Can't believe it. No sir, I just can't believe it."

Mr. Phillips called Mary in to make the arrangements for the couple. He gave her a brief overview of the situation and told her to find separate room.

Mary stammered. "But. . . sir."

It's Okay, Mary, put Molly in section two with the more active patients for now, that is until you can find her a room."

Joe's eyes sparkled and he grinned a mouthful of teeth. His dream had come true.

Molly had her own room with Myrtle, Joe had his dream come true and Mr. Phillips gladly turned the couple over to his social worker.

And they all lived happily ever after.

The Long Journey Home

Chapter One

Someone pounded on the door, swearing. The racket caused me to scrunch up in Mother's womb. She'd protect me.

Although I heard others say Father stood less than five- seven, people's talk said that he feared no man, liked the ladies too much and couldn't resist a good fight. I don't know what any of that meant, but if they are bad things I sure hope that changes before I'm born.

Nobody thinks of me as a real person yet. They don't know I can hear things and feel the outside world through Mother, but I really can. Like right now, I can hear pounding on the floor. I knew it had to be Father because Mother wasn't moving. Stomping makes him feel like a big person, I think. Suddenly I heard a different noise--so loud it echoed throughout the room and did-in my little ears. The screaming person with a low voice shouted words I don't dare repeat.

Mother stepped back, away from the sound. My space drew tight.

Father's voice didn't waiver when he answered the screaming person. "There's no need to get so bent out of shape," he said.

I could feel Mother's painful thoughts as she listened to the stranger. It had to be fear she felt because it happened once before when she told her parents about me. I remember Grandma yelling at Mother, but I don't think it had anything to do with us because she kept hollering Father's name—Charlie! So I figured it had to be something he had done.

"If you ever lay another hand on my wife, I'll kill you!" the screaming person shouted.

I felt Mother shake her head and rest her elbow on my foot. In this position I can only assume she placed her hand over her mouth in amazement. I did.

"I was only trying to be friendly for crying out loud."

Mother whispered, "Get the smug look off your face. You're asking to get beat up."

I didn't hear an answer from Father so I can only guess he didn't change anything.

I don't think that person ever spotted my hiding place, but his anger drew through Mother, pushing her into an invisible box. I was grateful. Then an internal whisper reached my little ears. *Isn't he going to deny it?* This time a magnitude of emotions flooded my space. Mother's heart had been broken and I was the only one who knew it. I stirred, weeping for my Mother.

"Who the hell do you think you are talking to—some jackass you little twerp? Putting your hand on my wife's ass is more than being friendly. I'm warning you—stay away from her or you're dead meat."

"Yeah! Yeah! Yeah!" Father said. Then a bang sounded and Father stomped again.

His voice had a shaky kind of laugh to it when he started to talk to Mother. "The guys a jerk! Just forget it. OK? I don't want to hear any more about it."

*   *   *

That's the way it all started, according to this baby. I don't remember a lot before this happened, but it wasn't long after before nature wanted to propel me right in to the world. I guessed Father knew because he asked Mother about going to a hospital. I had no idea what their plans were, I had to pay attention to mine. Without a doubt, I could feel something tightening right above my head. So I could hardly ignore it. I wasn't terribly concerned though, just a little uncomfortable. Of course I've been this way for some time. I'm upside down, you know. Besides, I've felt worse things when Mother was upset.

Father shouted that he'd call a cab—because we didn't have a car. I didn't know what either of those were, but I guessed I'd learn soon enough. It wasn't long after that he screamed at Mother to "get a move on." So I figured this cab thing must have come. I was pretty sure of it when I got squeezed as Mother bent over to crawl into something. Father grumbled about there being five people in the thing already. He whispered to Mother that the driver must be nuts, because he continued to go everywhere except this hospital place. I don't know why we had to go anywhere. I just wanted a nice soft place to land in.

That's about the time Father asked the driver if he wanted to deliver a baby. I supposed he was talking about me. Suddenly, this cab thing began to move a lot faster than I could. Back and forth it swayed as Mother clenched my space so tight I didn't have any breathing room.

By the time we got to the hospital, Mother was sick. The toast Father made her eat had spent too much time bouncing around in that cab. The nurse didn't help much either. She made Mother lie down when she wanted to sit up. Mother finished her off in a hurry when she gave the toast back to the nurse in worse condition than when it went down. After that the nurse let Mother do what she wanted—somewhat.

Just about that time I heard the nurse say Dr. Santangilo had shown up. Doc told Mother she had been in labor too long. I guessed I wasn't coming fast enough. He said he would have to rupture her membranes. Mother began to cry and crunch up even tighter than before.

"I won't hurt you," I heard him say. "I promise. In fact you won't even know I did anything."

I knew that wasn't going to fly, because I remembered the women at the USO talking about how horrible it was to have this done. One woman said she almost flew off the table from the pain. Besides, I didn't know what this meant to me. I didn't want to be jet-propelled into my new world, either. It took him awhile to convince both of us that we'd be safe during this rupture thing. Thankfully doc lived up to his word and Mother didn't see the spike he poked her with. But I did. Geepers Creepers! I'm sure glad I only have to go through this once.

Now it's the nurse's turn. I heard her tell Mother about a small swimming pool she wanted to put under her to catch the water. The only water I knew about I was floating in. So I figured that might be what she meant. She told Mother to let her know when she stopped leaking. I know I'm not very worldly at this point, but I couldn't figure out how Mother would know that.

Poor Mother, she lay on that thing so long I got a backache. Finally she couldn't stand it any longer and told the nurse she was finished. The nurse told Mother to get out of bed, so she could clean up the mess. Unfortunately, Mother's feet barely hit the floor when my space became a lot less wet. At about the same time I heard a gush and a splash when it all hit whatever the bottom was. Then the nurse screamed words that should've been added to the screaming person's vocabulary, not mine.

Mother cried inside. I felt sad.

Not long after that I slid into what Father called a condemned hospital under the direction of Dr. Santangilo. I watched the flies buzzing around doc's head as he held me upside down and slapped my behind.

Gee . . . I really thought I'd be right side up once I got here. Then he proceeded to suction every part of me—some I won't even mention. He weighed me in at five pounds on a cold scale. For the life of me, I don't know why Mother liked him so much. I didn't think those were nice things to do to a new person in this world.

Now the hospital was something else. A person didn't have to be there very long before they knew what the word condemned meant. I heard that there were only two nurses for the whole floor, maybe the whole hospital. I didn't know if that meant something good or bad at first, but then I got the feeling it wasn't good. Simply put, they kept getting confused about who should get what. The first thing had to do with an enema. It must have been a bad thing as Mother told the nurse, quite loudly, "Give it to her!" But from the sound of things that lady didn't want it either.

Maybe I'm getting ahead of my story, because that happened after the nurse told Mother to practice nursing until she got back. And I was hungry. All the nurse had given me was some water—more cruel and inhumane treatment.

I don't think Mother knew much about babies, because I heard her ask the nurse what to do with me. The nurse said, "Just let the baby suckle until I get back. The practice will do you good."

Mother continued to mind the nurse, trying to do the right thing. Of course that didn't do either of us any good, because the nurse didn't come back. By the time she did, Mother had started to cry. I wondered if I did something bad. Either way I didn't get any food for the rest of the day.

The next morning I woke up in my little bed to hear Dr. Santangilo screaming at the nurses. They had let me nurse too long and now Mother had blisters. Whatever those were I bet they were the reason I wasn't getting anything to eat. So you can see how I learned what the word condemned meant.

After several days in the hospital some unwelcomed news reached my little ears—my weight had dropped. Why wouldn't it? They were starving me to death. So I refused to smile or coo when they admired me. To get even, the nurse told Mother we'd have to spend another week in the hospital. I wanted to go home to my own new bed. At least I thought I did. That's before I knew about all the critters that crawled around the entire state of Georgia. So I'm thinking this hospital surely warned me about enough craziness to prepare me for my future journey. Ho-hum! I guess I'll learn to roll with the punches, just like mother.

Lace Curtains

I stood in the shadows in silence. Light spilled through the cobweb laced corners of the small basement windows and rested gracefully on the three card tables. A scuffed, oil cloth covered the tables and provided a work area for the ceramic creations. Miniature bottles of china paints were placed on the left side next to the tools and brushes. To the right rested a large block of clay kept moist with dampened clothes. The clay had to be kneaded to remove the air bubbles. Otherwise they could damage delicate pieces if they exploded and scattered particles throughout the kiln.

As mom worked meticulously over her work, her pompadour hairstyle of salt and pepper allowed streamers of silver to hang loosely around her hairline. With care, she rolled a clump of clay into a thin slab with an old rolling pin, and carved a petal for the rose with one of the needle-nosed cutting tools. She urged one petal after another with her fingertips to overlap the next until the rose found its final shape. Then she placed it on the vase. The work seemed repetitive, but mom didn't mind. She strived for the end result, perfection. On occasion I would wander into mother's workshop, amazed by her patience. *Could I create something so delicate?* Mom allowed me the silence of a brief watch to capture my curiosity. The temptation begged for participation. The stage set: I surrendered to rose formation, not knowing how it happened.

A perfect rose placed on a vase would be my model to follow. The child within giggled as I flattened the clay with the rolling pin. Silence held the room. The glimmer in mom's eyes told me she had faith in my ability. I had little. Back and forth I rolled a small piece of clay, like a child rolling out her first worm. I carved a petal; it seemed easy enough. Slow and certain movements would be required to remove a petal from the oil-cloth, without ruining its shape. I looked at mom's workspace to steal the secret; I sensed only patience.

Will I ever be able to do this? Determined I continued—for mom's sake—I told myself. Grumbling through the process, frustration soon led to more rolling, more carving and more tearing of the petals because I couldn't remove them from the cloth. *I need to be more inventive with my approach.* Lifting a partially damaged shape, I began to squeeze a petal into a form which left

15

finger marks of hills and valleys. In spite of its irregular appearance, I placed it on its worm-like base which had already begun to show signs of drying.

The fading light shimmered through the small basement windows. Evening soon would put an end to our work. My first rose lacked a convincing presentation.

Several times I had rerolled the clay, until a chalky dryness marked its form. *If I had kept the first one, I'd be finished by now.*

Discipline turned to defeat. I wadded the clay in my hand and plunked it down hard on the table; the tools and bottles jumped! My stomach tightened with shame. My efforts had not been rewarded with perfection, like my mother's.

Mom looked at me over her reading glasses with a thoughtful smile. "You must try to be more patient, dear. The clay is not to blame for what it becomes. The artist determines its design. Think of the clay as it is formed into rose petals. Now think of the events in your life. Each experience touches the last, just like the tiny petals that overlap.

We carry the knowledge we have gained from these experiences into the future, just like the vase displays the flowers. This in turn teaches us to think before we react, not to make the same mistakes, to plan our strategies and to understand our shortcomings.

For the artist, the end result is a solid foundation, a disciplined personality. For the clay, it is a beautiful rose. So it isn't just a piece of clay: it's a tool to help develop your future, one that can give you the patience you'll need to survive life's challenges. The choice is yours, sweetheart."

*   *   *

The years passed. The words spoken by mother remained in my heart to be carried into another realm. It happened when hard times hit my family, both food and money became scarce. Being raised by an affluent family, the bounty appeared like magic, but all that changed with an unfortunate marriage.

Month after month most monies for the family's bare necessities went toward what my husband called his needs. He said the pain kept him lame so he couldn't work much since the accident; he needed the money for hunting, fishing and cigarettes.

I asked how he could carry the heavy fishing gear or stand in the rapids, if his back hurt so much. With a cigarette hanging from his mouth, he said, "It helps me relax."

"But I could buy groceries for the children out of what's left," I argued.

He turned and walked out.

I didn't know what to do: I began to hide money, five dollars here, five dollars there. At mealtime I divided the food, making sure each child had a fair share. I didn't know if they went to bed hungry. I didn't ask. I didn't want to know. Yet, they cried when the man turned off the gas and the electric. They cried when the landlady told me she couldn't carry us any longer. They cried when we moved.

I struggled to trust God and His way, but it came hard. I needed a way to take care of my children. One night after I had put them to bed, I sat and wept.

In desperation I cried out. *I know I should have more patience while I wait for things in your time Father, but it's so hard with five children to feed. I've never asked you for anything except the piano, but I'm asking now. You know how hard things have been and how hard I've tried to be patient. But I can't wait any longer. I'm asking for my children, Father. Please! Christmas is only a few weeks away and we have nothing. Please don't forget them. We need you and love you so much. I beseech you Father . . . if it be your will. I ask this in Jesus' precious name.* I went to bed with hope in my heart, promising God I would be more patient. A whisper in my soul told me everything would be all right.

The next day, I received a call from the at-fault insurance company on my husband's accident case. "I had a feeling things were pretty rough for you and the family right now," the agent said. "I couldn't sleep last night thinking about it. I've decided to send you a thousand dollars. I hope that makes things a little easier for you and the children."

I almost dropped the phone when I heard his words. "Thank you! Thank you," I cried. "God bless you for your kindness and Merry Christmas."

Hanging up the phone, I fell to my knees. *Father, I thank you for this blessing. I know you sent this money for*

the children. I will see to it that's what it's used for . . . just
for the children.

* * *

The winter of my life had arrived. Another way emerged that demanded patience to keep the blessings alive. During the best part of my day, I allowed my thoughts to wander as I gazed through the lace curtains on the nursing home windows. Tall wooden stretchers used to stand in our backyard. They were nasty to the fingers with their needle-sharp pins protruding from their sides. I'd watch my grandma fill the washtub with a heavy-duty starch. Then mom would take the curtains from their bath to the backyard and put them on the stretchers. The ends of the curtains had to be attached to a pin, a painstaking task. Mother would tug and tug on the curtain until I thought the stretcher would snap. When she finished, the curtains were held in the grasp of the starch's rigidity, stiffening as they dried.

I don't remember the curtains being stiff when they came off the stretchers. I never felt them though. I wasn't allowed. You don't see the lace curtains as you go through life with a happy spirit. It's what's beyond them that you should see, like the snow on the hedges that changes a dreary day into the desire for hot chocolate heaped with clumps of marshmallows, or like that little girl kneeling next to her mother by the garden. What are they doing? Now I see—the mother has taken the child's hand in hers.

"There's nothing to be afraid of," she's telling the little girl. "Things in the soil can be good things."

I remember my mother telling me this very same thing when we sat by her garden. One day, she had bent forward and began digging a small hole. Suddenly she sat up. An earthworm, clumped with dirt, dangled from her fingers. I flinched! She lovingly put her arm around my shoulder. This did not comfort me in the least because it brought me too close to the worm.

"Oh no, sweetheart," she said. "Don't be afraid. He's a good little fellow. The worm helps make my flowers beautiful as it crawls around their roots. Why don't you make friends with him? He won't mind if you touch him."

I thought I'd try because mother would keep me safe. Slowly, I moved my finger toward the worm, touched it, giggled and my fear fled. The thought still makes my insides smile.

21

Now what am I hearing? There must be an organ grinder around here someplace. The music is so soft, far away. Maybe I'll see the man with the monkey. Oh, I'm sure I will. How I loved those monkeys when I was little. Grandma didn't. She said they were full of fleas, or worse yet, lice! Stay away from those monkeys, she'd holler out of the front door. I always minded her, but I didn't want to. Nowadays music sings in my head. Mother loved music, just like I do. I wonder if that little girl out there with her mother likes music.

The hallway door swung open. A breeze stirred the curtains, disturbing the moment. A familiar voice spoke from behind.

"OK, Mrs. B. It's time for your nap. You've been sitting in front of that window all day. I don't know what you're looking at. There's nothin' out there. Come on, sweetie."

Humiliation overpowered my patience with anger. *Don't call me that! I'm not your sweetie!* I wanted to scream it out loud, but I knew better. I needed to act like I had been molded into her idea of what I should be, or I wouldn't get to sit by the lace curtains any longer. With my patience being challenged, I didn't respond. Mother would be so proud. Right now I need to be just like the clay she used to make the roses— shaped into the likeness of what they expect me to be. But there aren't any roses here, only naps to keep me molded, quiet, and forgotten.

Swiftly, the aide swung the wheelchair toward the doorway: it squealed in defiance.

I wanted to say I didn't need a nap: that my world was on the other side of the lace curtains, but she'd just laugh and say, "It's time for your nap, sweetie." I wanted to say I saw life, but she'd just laugh and say, "It's time for your nap, sweetie."

The rigidity of her job has starched her just like the curtains on the stretcher. That's right, isn't it? I can see things more clearly now. My patience soars with the strength from my faith. Perhaps I could teach her about patience. I have a lot of experience.

Tomorrow I'll ponder this thought while I sit reminiscing by the lace curtains, holding on to my blessings.

Knock on Heaven's Door

The finger-tips of my kid gloves were frozen from the icy temperatures that had blown in from Lake Michigan. Indiana had never been so cold. Irritated, I slid my tape measure across the side of Mr. Bradley's home to get the dimensions for the appraisal. I hated doing appraisals, especially for divorces. Regardless it was work. So I stopped grumbling, roughly sketched the outer boundaries and put in the measurements for the calculations. The next day I did the finishing touches on the work and dropped it in the mail with my bill.

A month passed when I realized I hadn't received a check for the appraisal. Thinking it an oversight, I mailed another statement. A week later the appraisal came back from the client with a note. His attorney didn't need it, so he wasn't going to pay for it. I paged through the appraisal while my husband David watched.

"What's the matter, Honey?" he asked.

"The audacity of this man! Can you believe he returned my appraisal? Look! The pages aren't even in the same order. I bet he copied it, and now that he has what he wants he's refusing to pay for it. He must think I'm pretty stupid."

When Mr. Bradley hired me, he had made some bitter comments about his wife. My gut feeling was to refuse the job. Unfortunately, I allowed his "poor me" attitude to swayed me instead of listening to my instincts. Now I'd probably have to go to the court to collect my fee.

I began my crusade by repeatedly calling his body shop. The phone rang—his answering machine picked up. I left my name and number, but he never returned my calls. I sent another statement, trying to give him the benefit of the doubt. But that didn't work either. Not knowing what else to do, I filed in small claims court. Three months later I showed up for court, but the defendant didn't.

"Now what?" I asked the clerk of courts.

Her monotone voice and expressionless look never changed. "Well, since he didn't appear, you automatically win the case."

"I mean how do I collect?"

She pulled out a brochure and handed it to me with a sigh of disinterest. "Here's the protocol for the follow up. The system works, if you don't give up."

"Why this could take six months, maybe more."
The words "it's the principle of the thing" ran through the charged part of my mind. *He's not going to get away with this, no matter how long it takes.*

"Give me the forms!"

*   *   *

Another winter passed. Even though I had followed the courts procedures, I wasn't any closer to getting my money than when I walked out of court. I had held onto my principles until they were choking the life out of my other real estate business. In spite of what the clerk said, the time involvement confirmed that I should give up the aggravation.

One day after getting the mail, I noticed David's checkbook on the front seat of my car. When I picked it up, a piece of paper fell out with Mr. Bradley's name on it. Knowing that David had some body work to be done on his truck, I rushed into the house to tell him not to do business with this man.

"For heaven sake, David, what are you doing with Mr. Bradley's name? Certainly you weren't planning to take the truck to him, were you?"

He looked at me strange, sort of awkward, and said, "I can't tell you right now, just trust me. Oh, I see you got the mail."

"Why?" I waited for his answer while I paged through the mail.

He smiled as he pointed to a letter. "Hmm, I believe that one is for you."

Questioning his surety with a curious glance, I opened the letter and found a check for the appraisal from Mr. Bradley. I stood in disbelief, thinking it would probably bounce. "Now I can tell you," David said. "I've been writing to his angel. Every time you have a person who needs prayers or won't pay his bill, like this fellow, you can write to his angel."

"Where in the world did you get such an idea?"

"Gee! I really don't know. I started doing it years ago." He laughed and said, "I guess God told me about it."

With the check in my hand, I listened to David share his personal communication with our Father. My skepticism turned to wonderment.

Then he began to write his model letter.

"To the Angel of

_____(name)_____, I write.

I ask that _____(name)_____angel

brings God's abundance to him, blessing him with the

wealth of the universe. I know that he is an honest and

trustworthy man who understands fairness. I thank his

angel for helping ___(name)_____ to understand

his responsibility in paying for the appraisal he requested.

If it be your will, I ask this in Jesus'

name that you bless _____

(name)_____angel for his help in obtaining

this favor.

Signed:_____."

     The key is to clearly state what you want the person

to do, and believe that our Father will handle it. That's it!

Now—tear it up, throw it away and forget about it. You

have to do this every morning for seven days, unless you

get results before then." David's eyes glistened as he shared

his belief. "You look surprised. It really works. All you

have to do is look at the check in your hand to know that."

Amazed by this simple prayer, David's expectations and the check in my hand, I didn't know what to say. All this time I had been struggling with the hard-nosed policies of the court system. If I had given the job to God, my life would've been a lot simpler. That'll teach me to go to a higher court in the future.

On the Road Again

The humid air heightened the shriek of the whistle as my brother Harry pushed the alarm. Dad had taken off again. Men and women hurriedly shut down their machines, grabbed their car keys, and ran out the door.

"Which way do you think he went this time?" Someone shouted over the whining of the machines as they grinded to a halt.

"I'm not sure," Harry yelled. "I just know that he's not in the john and I can't find him anywhere. So let's get out and start looking. And don't forget to check the bakery first."

Since my husband had taken ill, I had to work at Harry's plant over the summer to pay my family's expenses. As I hadn't seen my dad for several months, I wasn't familiar with his latest antics. Surprised by the happenings, I walked to the doorway of the plant and watched as workers jumped into their cars and rushed off in different directions.

"Does he do this often?"

A frown creased Harry's forehead as he stood with hands on hips, nodding. "Yeah! Every time he gets it in his

30

head that he can get a better paying job someplace else. It's a wonder he can work at all, being half paralyzed, much less hit the road in that beat up wheelchair. Half the time I'm worried that he'll get hurt on a piece of machinery, and the other half the crew is out looking for him. I guess he must be sick of taping those boxes. And who wouldn't be? I better start him on something else. Maybe the paper machine will keep him happy for a while. We'll have to watch him pretty close so he doesn't get his good hand caught in it. Have to run. We'll talk when I get back."

An hour later Harry arrived at the plant, pushing Dad in his wheelchair. As he passed my machine, Harry rolled his eyes and shook his head. Elbows tucked in, Dad sat round-shouldered with a smirk at the end of the glasses that had slid down his nose.

Entrepreneurial blood ran through the veins of this man who had been reduced to folding boxes for a living with his one good arm. Eight hours a day, Dad would transform a flat piece of cardboard into a box with the left side of his body. Then he'd secure the bottom with tape so that it could be used for packing the corners of the aluminum siding.

Wheeling Dad around to face him, Harry knelt down: "Dad, I can't keep shutting the plant down to look for you. This time it was way too dangerous. You were on a major highway headed toward Milwaukee, for crying out loud. How in the world did you get so far away from Hartland? Never mind, I don't want to know. All I know is you're going to put me out of business, if you keep this up."

Dad grunted and rubbed his left thumb and index fingers together.

"What do you want—a raise?"

Dad nodded.

"OK, fine! If I give you a promotion with it will that keep you here?"

A sparkle lit Dad's eyes.

"Good! You can work on the paper machine for a few weeks to see if you can handle it."

Before Dad's stroke, our Irish mother used to say that his hallmark was the wide-brimmed hat that dipped down over his soft, smiling eyes along with the "blarney" that came from his German mouth. In spite of that, she marveled at his sense of humor and knew his good heart, as did the workers at his woolen mills. Every day he would go through the mill to make sure things were safe. He was never too proud to work alongside a laborer or afraid to save someone who had caught his hand in a machine. Because of this, people would seek his favor, offering to work longer hours without pay to meet the deadlines for the blankets the army needed during WWII.

When the mill burned down in 1948, Dad was forced to take a job, working double shifts seven days a week in his brother's factory to support our family. Even though Dad was responsible for his brothers' wealth, neither of them could find a suitable job for him in the office. Instead, Dad was ordered to increase production in their plant. He began to run several machines at a time, standing in cold rooms until his legs were numb, lying on concrete floors, attempting to repair worn machines that should have been discarded years before. The drudgery continued for several years until at age fifty-nine he was stricken with a massive heart attack and a stroke.

I remember standing at the bedside of a person who vaguely resembled my father. Paralysis held his entire right side with a firm grip. His stocky erect physique had been reduced to eighty pounds, leaving his body withered. There was nothing I could do except watch as the stroke twisted his limbs into painful contractions. Mother held her vigilant, looking tired and troubled. I remained fearful.

My upbringing only included smiling at a handicapped person, never dealing with one. I couldn't accept that he would be a cripple. My dad was my hero. Who would fill that role now?

Each visit became more stressful because of my lack of understanding. When he tried to talk, only garbled sounds spurted from his mouth. I wanted to run from the room, but stayed. Mother would be upset if I left. He'd point at things that he wanted. I struggled for the answer, but never seemed to get it right. I wished there were some rules or clues on how to behave around a stroke victim, but no, nothing. Instead I dwelt on what I had lost, not on what my father had lost.

Growing up, I saw my dad as a fun-loving person who delighted in changing the rules to see if anyone would catch him in the act. Often his shenanigans got him in trouble, like the time he had played Sheepshead with the family. He didn't follow suit and held back his trump.

Realizing what he had done, the green came out of my Irish mother and flattened his humor. He had ruined her no-trick hand. She said she'd never play with him again. I'm not sure if she ever did.

The pranks that Dad had used on my five older siblings were well polished by the time they got to me. These, of course, brought more than a smirk from my siblings as they became engrossed in dad's favorite antics. Almost every night at the dinner table, Dad would sample my milk, chuckle as he watched my expression and then ask, "Hello, little girl. What's your name?"

My face flushed as I gritted my teeth, trying to give a somewhat polite answer. He continued this irritating behavior for years. Then one day after I was married, he decided to resurrect the question, trying it on my three year old son, Rory.

"What's your name, little boy?"

"Rory," he responded politely as he continued to eat his cereal.

A moment passed and Dad repeated the question. A quizzical look crossed Rory's face as he turned toward his grandfather. All the same, he repeated his answer, only this time much louder: "Rory!"

From years of practice, Dad knew he was beginning to get to Rory. So he tried one more time, "What's your name little boy?"

Rory turned sharply toward his grandfather and enunciated clearly, "Rory! What's the matter with you? Can't you remember from one minute to the next?"

Appalled by Rory's response, I rushed across the room to correct him, but before I could do anything, Dad broke into hearty laughter.

"Now that's a smart kid! That kid has some spirit!"

I stood amazed. After all those years of answering that stupid question, he simply wanted to see how much good old-fashioned spunk I had.

*   *   *

After months of hospitalization, Dad had grown strong enough to go home. Within a year, he had mastered most of his daily care with the support of Harry and Mom. His new freedom intact, he wanted a job. Harry obliged. Every morning Harry bolted into my parents' home around 6:30 and literally swirled Dad around in his wheelchair and out the front door. Dad was always dressed and waiting. He had a job to go to and an income to earn. Often I wondered what might cause him to take off in his wheelchair now and then during the ten years he worked at the plant. I had a feeling that it wasn't entirely to get a better job, but rather that he might have been toying with Harry.

As time passed, my fears diminished in the wake of his courage. His love for life had shaped my destiny. Dad didn't give up when adversity struck. He continued to live the best that he could, teaching me that I could chose to look to the humor in life instead of the darkness. I could laugh out loud often, cherish every moment, and never give up. And if that didn't work, I could always tease the grandchildren.

Sometimes I told an exaggerated story about a man driving down the road, and being passed by an old man in a self-propelled, broken-down wheelchair. Everyone saw it as a monumental joke until they learned the truth. This beautiful spirit, with his wide-brimmed hat dipped down over his soft, smiling eyes was *on the road again*, looking for the best that life had to offer.

Tall Tales

Her arm circled several times, she drew back and throw the ball with a mighty thrust to her imaginary opponent. Her grandmother watched Katie for a few moments, laughing at her ten year old granddaughter's antics.

"Katie," her grandmother shouted as she approached the pitcher's mound. "Do you play ball at school?"

"Yeah, I do, Grandma," she said as she readied herself for another pitch. "I have a really good arm. That's why I'm the pitcher."

"Maybe you should be an outfielder. They can always use someone with a good arm in the outfield—they have to be able to throw a ball a long way."

Katie's pitch immediately changed to an overhead cast to demonstrate her good arm.

"I used to play ball when I was a girl," Grandma said.

With a hint of surprise, Katie yelled, "No way!"

"Yes, I was a catcher, just like my dad. I never had much trouble in that position except for this one girl who always threw her bat. I'd tried to jump out of its way, but a couple of times it landed right across my shins. That hurt so bad I wanted to cry. Well, I couldn't do that in front of everybody, so I got dang angry instead. I put my face square in hers and said, you throw that bat one more time and I'm going to turn you inside out."

All movement stopped. Katie's eyes widened and her jaw dropped. "Really! That's what you told her?"

"You betcha!"

"Boy, that's something, Grandma."

After a moment of silent contemplation, they began walking toward the house.

"Do you know what happened to my dad when he was a catcher? He would've been your great-grandpa."

Staring up at her grandma, Katie shook her head.

"Too bad you never got to meet him because he was sure a character."

Stopping, she turned toward Katie. "Well…let me tell you about it. Your great-grandpa apparently got himself in a heap of trouble as a catcher."

"He did?"

"Yes, he did!"

"Now picture this. The umpire hollers, 'batter up.' The crowd cheers. A heavyset man stomps to the plate swinging his bat back and forth. Now mind you, the catcher, your great-grandpa, places his mitt dead center behind the plate. The pitcher's arm begins to twirl. He hunches back and throws the ball. As soon as the batter connects, he lets his bat go flying from his hands. The crowd grows silent when the bat hits your great- grandpa right across the forehead, so hard . . . both of his eyes popped out."

"EEEEWWW!" Katie squealed.

"I know. I could hardly believe it myself. Poor great-grandpa, there he stood, looking at the ground when he thought he was looking straight ahead. Can you imagine that?"

"Oh my gosh!" moaned Katie.

"Of course great-grandpa went straight to the doctor and they put his eyes back in as easy as pie. It's told that he never had a problem after that, either. Now remember," she laughed. "I said your great-grandfather was a character, so I often wondered if his tales held even a smidgeon of truth to them."

Katie giggled as she walked toward the house, "Probably not, Grandma. That's a pretty big fish to swallow."

Grandma got into her car with a masked smile, wondering if there really was any truth to his stories. She couldn't be certain, knowing her dad. Nevertheless, his stories were not easily forgotten and she told them over and over again to make sure. Maybe this one would be passed on to the next generation, like his other infamous grandpa stories.

The Latest Guest

Late Friday afternoon, the sweet smell of baby-back ribs roasting in the oven filled our tri-level home with a tantalizing, spicy aroma. Mom had just finished basting them with her homemade barbecue sauce and turned them as she did. I watched closely. I wanted to make sure I learned her secrets.

My name is Mary Elizabeth. I'm twelve, almost thirteen. I'm the oldest of mom's five kids, so mom named me after my great-grandma. She lived with us ever since my great-grandpa died. The stories I heard mom tell about great-grandma when she was a girl will keep us laughing for a long time.

Great-grandpa loved to take mom to the track and teach her about horseflesh. I hear tell she was only about three the first time they went. With her hand in his, they'd walk to the stables and he'd point out the important parts of the horse, like its spirit, the shape of its rump and the depth of its chest. He must have been a good teacher because mom's horses usually came in first. Mom said that great-grandpa would look at her sort of funny, scratch his bald head and laugh. I guess he never could figure out how mom picked those winners. My sister Jodi is not quite eleven months younger than me. I don't know where she is right now, seems she always disappears whenever there's work to be done.

My brothers are in their bedroom, finishing their homework. That'll be the day. Jimmy, the oldest boy, who comes after Jodi, actually pretends the bunks beds are silos. Once I peeked through a crack in the door to see what he was doing. There he was climbing up the ladder on the bunk-bed, like a pirate on an old ship. Then he'd leap from one bed to the other. Of course, Tommy and Joey couldn't let their big brother have all the fun, so they'd play follow the leader. It's a wonder there are any springs left in those beds, any curtains on the windows, or that they didn't come crashing through the ceiling.

Mom pretty much ignores them until she can't stand it anymore. Then she'll go stomping up the stairs to correct them. I think mom stomps, so they'll hear her coming up the steps and quiet down some, but it hasn't worked yet. I can't say as though I blame her for trying to ignore them because within seconds of her saying her piece, they are right back at it again. It'll be a miracle if they get their homework done before we leave for the camping trip. Come to think of it, I wouldn't be surprised if mom made them take it along. That would teach them a lesson and make my day.

"Mary Elizabeth! Could you please check the ribs in a few minutes while I get some of this laundry put away and try to settle your brothers down?"

"Sure Mom."

"Your dad will be home any minute and I haven't begun to pack for the trip."

I knew the laundry had to be taken care of before we could go any place. So I began to fold and stack it as I looked out our bay window. Charlie, our full grown white duck, was waddling around lazily, pulling tuffs of grass out of the lawn for his afternoon snack. He had plenty of schmaltz on him, as great-grandma used to say, and it sure slowed him down when he went on a rampage after the boys. Of course, that happened almost every day. Those boys just couldn't leave that duck alone. I wouldn't tell mom this, but I was glad when Charlie got a hold of one of them, or pulled their hair when they fell down.

Frankly, it was a relief to have only one animal to look after. Every time we turned around, dad would bring home a stray or some half dead animal he found along the roadside. Size didn't matter either, anything from a tadpole to a horse.

At least most of them were harmless, like the dove with a broken wing. Mom didn't know about the bird until she got up to make breakfast and saw it. There it sat on a broom stick balanced between two chairs in her kitchen. That was unfortunate for dad. I don't know who looked more shocked, the bird or mom. Dad had splinted its wing with a flat piece of wood and then wrapped it with adhesive tape. That one jerked my brain around some—wouldn't the feathers come off with the tape? Well . . . nobody seemed to want to answer that question.

"Get that bird out of my kitchen!" Mom screamed.

Obviously, she was not happy.

"Where am I supposed to put it then?" Dad grumbled.

That must have been one of those rhetorical sentences because I don't think he wanted an answer.

Carolee O'Neill

My dad stretched out came to about five foot six, but he could throw a side of beef around, so he wasn't weak. Of course, that's until mom hollered at him.

"I don't care," Mom yelled. "Just get it out of my kitchen. I will not cook and feed the children with a bird next to the table, pooping on the floor!" Now, I love birds, but that thing was a little much. Every morning it would serenade us way before we had to get up. By the time it was well enough to fly, the family was talking about having it for dinner.

But some things dad brought home were downright dangerous, like the one eyed owl that attempted to land on us with its claws spread. More than once Mom grabbed whatever she could to swat it away from us, but let me tell you that was one smart bird. Somehow it would pick the lock on its cage and out he'd come. Unfortunately, we never knew where he hid himself.

Hunting for a one-eyed owl when you're trying to get ready for school is not nifty. Sometimes I feared I'd be the one to find it, or worse yet he'd find me first. The Christmas tree seemed to be his favorite spot. That made sense. He'd get himself way back by the trunk, which made

46

it impossible to grab him without getting clawed. He'd sit there, swiveling his head and blinking the one good eye. Then he'd start to hop toward the front of the tree and we'd go screaming in all directions. That went on until one day Jodi went whining to mom that the owl was laying on its back with its feet in the air. I thought I heard Mom whisper "Thank heavens!" Of course it was dead, but Jodi didn't know that. Then we had to have a funeral for a bird that almost clawed our eyes out.

Now the baby skunk, that thing almost got dad a divorce. Sure the skunk was cute. And dad *thought* it was deodorized. He said the guy that sold it to him said so. I don't know how you check a skunk to see if it's not going to squirt you, and I don't want to know. When I looked at Mom, she stood with her hands on her hips, her mouth wide open and her eyes looked like they were ready to pop out of her head.

"You mean you paid for that thing? What are you, nuts or something?"

On that note, dad and the skunk made a hasty retreat, right out the front door.

"And don't come back with anything else! This is absolutely the last straw!"

I wish I could say dad listened to mom's threats, but his good behavior usually didn't last more than a day. I better get busy and get those ribs basted. Mom had barely finished folding the laundry, when I heard the kitchen door slam and dad holler, "Mary Elizabeth, look what I brought home!"

It was one of those times when I was glad to be on the first floor because those boys came flying out of their room like a herd of buffalo. They pushed and shoved each other from one side of that staircase to the other, hoping to be the first to see what dad had saved this time. Mom stood at the top of the stairs with her arms folded across her chest. She wasn't smiling.

Between my rowdy brothers and sister, I saw a puppy.

When mom arrived at the scene of the crime, she stood speechless with her hand over her mouth. I could see why she didn't know what to say. This puppy was as cute as a dog could be. Dad waved the supposed papers and shouted that it was a full-blooded German shepherd already housebroken. I've seen lots of dogs over the years, mostly because dad brought them home. So my experience told me the puppy couldn't have been more than six weeks old. He was black, except for light-brown markings on his face, chest and front legs, and his ears were standing straight up.

Mom still wasn't smiling.

Panting, the dog's dark eyes flashed back and forth between us. The light caught the blackness of his eyes as he sat, softening her heart. Then he cocked his head to one side with his left upper lip tucked into his mouth, and looked at Mom as if to say, "Aren't you going to say hello?" The usual scream of "get this thing out of the house" obviously had left her thoughts.

"Come on, Mom," Jimmy coaxed. "He's so neat and soft and happy. When he grows up he can protect you. Come on, Mom, pet him. You're going to love him."

Mom listened to Jimmy's sales pitch until she smiled. Jimmy's snow-white hair, contrasted with his deep suntan, seemed to make his grin even broader.

Mom knelt down and gently squeezed the dog's face and held it up to hers.

"Well now, what are we going to name you?"

It sounded like dad let all of the air out that he'd been holding.

Tommy shouted, "How about Sam?" His crystal-blue eyes sparkled as his slender six year old body jumped up and down. Naming the dog certainly meant we were going to keep him.

"No, I don't like that!" pouted chubby, little Joey.

I figured at three and a half he didn't know why, except he didn't get to pick the name.

"Henry!" Mom said. "We're going to call you, Henry, after my grandpa."

Looking at us, she added, "You know your great-grandpa was an Irishman with a good attitude and just enough devil in him to make life interesting. I think this Henry has the same little devil in him and his personality seems to flourish, almost with a smile. How does that sound to everyone?"

"That's good!" Jimmy shouted excitedly, then he looked at the rest of us. "Henry! Mom likes that name, so that's what it's going to be."

I tell you, the grin on Jimmy's face could have melted an iceberg, especially when I heard him whisper, "Gee, thanks, Mom!"

"Well then, Henry, welcome to your new home."

We all fell in love with Henry, especially Mom. Henry was absolutely the classiest puppy and utterly adorable. I'm sure that I saw tears in Mom's eyes when she lovingly stroked the back of our latest guest, but I don't know why. Maybe it had something to do with her grandpa.

Sinister Secrets

Ominous, gray clouds drifted toward a small town in Nebraska; bells tolled in the distance. Beth Bracken sat quietly in her favorite wingback chair in the dimly lit living room. Slowly, she turned the pages of the old photo album that lay on her lap with its faded, yellowed pictures of yesteryear.

Mama always put me in such pretty little dresses. I couldn't help I kept tearin' the sashes. I was just playin'.

Beth's fingertips caressed the faces on her pictures as though they were alive. *Thirty-two curls I used to have. Yeah. Every night Mama would roll my hair in little pieces of rags, and the next day she'd make thirty-two curls. You'd think with all that rollin' and curlin' some of it would've stayed. But no, my mousy brown hair is just as straight as ever.*

A little twitched, but harmless was the gossip Beth heard whispered behind her back. The slow, but sweet one, they called her. Beth's eyes focused on a picture of her husband Leo.

Slapping the face of the picture, she snickered sadistically. *You think I don't know what you were doin'?*

Ha! What a naughty, naughty man you are. I told Mama what you were doin.' She told me to get away from you as fast as I could. But I had a better idea. 'Dem bones, 'dem bones are goin' walk around, 'dem bones, 'dem bones are gonna walk around. That'll give you somethin' to think about.

Wonder who else will show up in here. Oh, there's Mama. She looks so good in her blue dress and her hair all done up. Now she hardly ever does her hair, 'cause she's all bent over and her hands ache. She never did like Leo. I should've listened to her. She said he was no good from the start. And here's Auntie Kate. She's always been so good to me, buyin' me little gifts and takin' me places. This book is so old it even smells old, just like granddad's room after he'd been smokin' cigars. I don't know why Mama keeps putting' new pictures in this old book.

Well, look it here, another good for nothin'. And you were supposed to be my best friend. Everybody knew what you were doin'. They said I didn't, because I'm not all there. But I knew what was goin' on. And I'm not crazy…I'm not! Then you went and said you loved us both. Why, you could make a person crazy with what you were doin'. That bleached blond hair and tight dress won't do you no good no more, 'cause it's too late.

Pulling the picture from its slot, Beth ripped it to shreds, threw the fragments across the room, and slid the album haphazardly onto the coffee table. She sat and sulked for a moment. Then she realized the bells had stopped tolling.

I guess they'll be comin' out of that church soon. Mama went and told all those people to come over here after the service. Why did she have to go and do that? Now they'll expect me to wait on 'em and listen to 'em talk about the gory details of her death.

People just love to talk about how other people died. Seems we need more funerals around here.

Hat in hand, Marilyn bolted through the front door, calling to her daughter, "They're right behind me, Beth! Come on! We've got to get things ready."

Marilyn glanced quickly around the room, "Haven't you done anything while I was gone? I thought I told you to set the tables up and start the coffee. And what are all these little snibbles of paper on the floor? Oh...never mind, I'll do it myself. I should've known better than to expect you to get anything done."

Beth grimaced at her mother's attack. Offended, she grabbed a card table, forced its legs outward to make it stand up. "I don't know why you had to invite all 'em people over here, anyway. Why didn't you take 'em to your house?"

"Oh Beth, stop complaining. Becky just lost her only daughter, for pity sake. I can't very well deal with my best friend's loss and prepare for a wake too, now can I?"

Marilyn's speech became choked. Her eyes filled with tears as she tried to press the images of Judy's death from her mind. "It's not as though she died of natural causes, you know. That would've been bad enough. But to be mutilated the way Judy was…Dear God. It's no wonder her mother is crazy with grief."

"She ought to be, raisin' a kid like that. She was rotten right down to her core."

Outraged, Marilyn rebuked, "I can't believe you said that. Don't you have any feelings for anyone else?"

Boldly, Beth sneered at her mother as she picked up a boning knife, gliding her thumb across the blade. "Not for the likes of her I don't."

Appalled by her daughter's behavior, Marilyn yelled, "I haven't got time to deal with you right now. We'll finish this conversation later."

The doorbell rang, causing Marilyn to falter and straighten her dress. Still looking over her shoulder in contempt at Beth, she opened the door. Staring blankly at the ghost-like face of her friend Becky; her thin, frail torso accented by the blackness of her garb. Only the end of her pinched nose showed the grief that she bore.

"Oh...Becky," Marilyn cried. "Do come in. Please make yourself at home. The chair over there by the fireplace is very comfortable, and if it is too close to the fire, we could move it."

Streams of women, dotted by an occasional husband, followed closely behind Becky. "Where should we put the food?" hollered Aunt Kate as she walked straight to the kitchen. The robust woman wore a threadbare outfit that looked as though it had been to too many funerals. She smiled at Beth, throwing her a kiss. Then she finished preparing her food and set it on the table.

The ritual began. People, with selected morsels, paraded past Becky, offering their condolences. Gathered in one corner, guests whispered with enthusiasm about how the crime had been committed and who was the guilty party. Some speculated that a jealous boyfriend in a rage could've commit this hideous crime; or else it had to be someone who knew Judy pretty well. How else would a person have gotten into the house? There weren't any signs of a struggle. Some worried that someone in their community could actually have done such a thing. No one was safe, not even in their own homes.

The room darkened as thunder rumbled and a flash of lightening set the stage for the impending storm. The air drew heavy with a cool dampness, planting the seed that someone else could meet with the same violent death. Hurriedly, guests left, hoping to escape their worries.

Realizing what had happened, Marilyn hastened to Becky's side, and helped her to her feet, "Time, Becky, time. That's what you need. Why don't you come and help me in the kitchen? It might keep your mind off of things."

Debris cluttered the tables and counters of the Bracken home after the guest had departed. Half full cups, crumpled napkins, silverware encrusted with food, and the smell of burnt coffee hung in the air. Clouds gave way to their weight; flashes of lightening cast bizarre shadows over the uneaten food on the china plates.

* * *

Beth begrudgingly cleared the tables—her thoughts turned to Leo's indiscretions. *My stomach feels so sick inside when my head thinks of him, like I wanna throw up, but can't. I'm tired of cryin' over what he does. No use, anyway. It won't stop till I'm dead. That's what I'm feelin' like, dead inside, just like that corpse.*

She began to weep softly. When she heard the back door slam, she quickly wiped her tears from the corners of her eyes with the back of her hand.

"What's for supper?" Leo hollered.

"Suit yourself. I'm not cooking nothin' else," Beth shouted from the dining room. "Mama went and left me with this mess to clean up from that wake. I don't need to be making more on top of it."

"Well, I don't care what you've been doin', I want some supper," Leo yanked a chair from under the table and dropped his middle-aged body on it.

Beth glared at him. "Why don't you just go over to one of your livin' girlfriend's places, and have her dish you up something long and skinny?"

"What the hell is that supposed to mean?" he yelled.

"If the shoe fits, wear it. I ain't saying nothin' more." She turned her back to him and began walking toward the living room.

Clenching his fist, he quickly walked to catch up to her. He screeched at the top of his voice, "What's this? Some more of your half-witted thinkin'? What do you do all day sit and dream up trouble? A man can't even come home for supper without being accused of some crazy, off beat crap. I'm tired, and I want some supper, I said. Now get your ass out in that kitchen and start cookin'."

Leo grabbed Beth's arm, digging his fingernails deep into her flesh. He dragged her into the kitchen and released his grip with a final shove. She struggled to keep her balance, but her feet slipped. Anguish twisted her face as she fell against the kitchen counter, upsetting the china stacked by the sink. Beth, along with the china, tumbled to the floor. She cried out as plates of all sizes shattered around her. When the last plate had fallen, she pulled herself into a kneeing position in the wasted treasures.

Leo sneered.

"Not grandma's dishes," she moaned. *Mama will be mad 'cause they're all she had left.*

Blood oozed from her fingertips as she picked up one piece after another and tried to match the jagged edges. When she realized her efforts were in vain, she cried out viciously. "Why did you go and do this? Why do you always have to hurt somebody?"

"I can't help you're so clumsy," Leo retorted smugly, disregarding her anguish.

Pain racked, she pulled herself up next to the sink, placing the broken pieces in her hand on the counter.

Leo turned and opened the refrigerator.

The boning knife lay on the counter. She picked it up, hiding it behind her back.

"Don't play no games with me, Mr. Bracken," she growled.

Hearing the harshness in her voice, Leo momentarily glanced over his shoulder, shrugged, and turned back toward the refrigerator.

"I knew what you were doin' with all 'em girls you brought home. You think I don't have no feelins', don't yeah? I'd sit up all night waitin' for you to come home. I'd cry until my face puffed up and I couldn't blow my nose no more. And you—where were you? You were out strokin' their long hair and buyin' them clothes. If you're so tired, Mr. Bracken, maybe you should go lay down or somethin'. Maybe you need a nice long nap."

The End.

Carolee O'Neill

Chocolate

From Silly to Sinister. A Short Story Collection

The Carolee Collectables

by Carolee O'Neill

Goodie RudeShoes: Series One, children 5 to 100.
Billy BitterBetter: Series Two, children 5 to 100.
Granny NeatFreak: children 4 to 100.
The Mouse House: children 4 to 100.
That Secret Part of Me: children 3 to 100.
From Silly to Sinister Short Stories:
Book One and Two.
Fiction for teens through mature adults.
Navigating the Potholes of Life:
Fiction for teens and adults.
adventure, comedy, drama.
A Reason to Dream:
Fiction for teens and adults,
a drama based on a true story.
Three versions of The Graduation.
The Graduation: A stand-alone novel
for teens through mature adults.
The Graduation with Study Guide.
for parents with teens, teens and adults.
The Graduation Study Guide
for those who prefer a separate copy of the guide.
Fiction: suspense, humor, insightful.
With God in Mind.
Thought provoking prose
for teens through mature adults.

Carolee can reached at: caroleeagain1934@gmail.com
http://books2c4kids.com

Carolee's books are available as paperback and as ebooks.
Thank you for your interest in my work.

Carolee O'Neill

From Silly to Sinister. A Short Story Collection

Carolee O'Neill

www.ingramcontent.com/pod-product-compliance
Lightning Source LLC
Chambersburg PA
CBHW061453170626
46811CB00004B/1492